Bagdad Is Everywhere

Poems 1984–1991

by

Michael Thorpe

TSAR
Toronto
1991

The publishers acknowledge generous assistance
from the Ontario Arts Council and the Canada Council,
and from the Bell Faculty Fund, Mount Allison University.

ISBN 0-920661-20-3

TSAR Publications
P.O. Box 6996, Station A
Toronto, M5W 1X7   Canada

Cover design: Rossitza Skortcheva Penney
Author photo: Thaddeus Holownia

Acknowledgements

Most of these poems have appeared or are accepted to appear in:

The Abegweit Review, The Antigonish Review, The Cormorant, Country Life (UK), *CV II, The Dalhousie Review, Doors* (UK), *Encounter* (UK), *Focus on Robert Graves and His Contemporaries* (US), *Foxtail* (US), *Germination, The Literary Half-Yearly* (India), *The Literary Review* (UK), *Outposts* (UK), *The Pottersfield Portfolio, The South Eastern Review, The Toronto South Asian Review, Third Eye* (UK), *Westwords* (UK), *Wild East.* Some are reprinted from *Animal Relations* (Salamanca Chapbooks, Fredericton).
"Maple and Boy" was First-Prize poem in the Writers' Federation of New Brunswick Poetry Competition, 1988.

For Elin

Contents

I

RUSKIN'S PINE

...how utterly different the impression of such a scene would be, if it were in a strange land, and one without history; how dear to the feeling is the pine of Switzerland compared to that of Canada.
                    Ruskin's Diary, 1846.

We know what Ruskin felt and meant, how long
Human endeavour steeped that Swiss scene:
In historyless places there can be no high-thinking
Tourists, first-comers beat out every path;
Before theirs, no eyes have seen, no hand grasped
This threaded stone, assembled crackling cones
For a wayside blaze. There *is* no way.

Fancy now that the first imprint
Must be your own, there is nothing
To reflect back upon, all must be
Your primal making, you will merge with
The fantasy of history–whose pine
Will be irradiated by the gaze of generations,
Sensed in ancestral communion:

They will invent you, the first seer,
And you must lose yourself to become
History's eye upon that pine,
The essential pioneer your heirs imagine.

HERE

This dawn, at five, crows
Bark, presumptuous,
Command clarifying space,
An undertone of sparrows
Their murmuring subjects.
Beyond maple candelabra
The sky washes its canvas,
Shames chill green saucers
Of municipal lamps,
And now the sun prints
A mellow grid upon the wall,
Bars of no unloved cell:
Rise and look down–
The cat waits in a brown study,
The crows switch off, and then
The first car
Bound nowhere.

MAPLE AND BOY

I accepted at last that of twelve upswept
limbs composing my maple candelabrum
four be cut away: then a slight youth
commanded the fork of the massive tree,
balanced as on the spars
of a grand clipper at sea,
on his toes tore at the cord
of a chainsaw whose least false jolt
might slice arm or leg and drain
his blood-sap into the sawdust he'd sown,
but the boy's steady skill avoided wounds,
whose surgery may renew life beyond his—
though to him it is just another tree
and he to it not even a boy:
each to the other indifferent, perfectly,
each accomplished beauty, cut to the life.

THE ROCK MAPLE'S END

1
The lengthening days' light
etches each familiar sight:
as Earth absorbs grey snow
we absolve the harsh season–
and again find reason
to begin to believe
in something new; yet
our massive centenarian
will again put on less green
this May, continue to die
against feathering skies...

2
It threw up blossom–and
we hoped–which stiffened,
did not open: no leaf.
Its last act was to madden
the driven saw and blunt
the screaming chain.
Now birds dash through
its overthrown fiefdom;
in vain the eye prints
that great invisible tracery
upon a fallen sky...

MONODY IN PIONEER'S REST

Neighbourly journals and deep-feeling poets
still find more than enough words for death,
but monumental styles have turned reticent:
mere records mostly of names and dates--
a living spouse's awaits termination–
the stones are hunched, they never soar.
Have the ancient slogans of peace and rest
come to seem dead letters mailed without end?
Have immortal longings narrowed to this–
stern-eyed acceptance or resignation,
fodder for sociological investigation?
One could hazard it hints a transition
to some stoical time when all corpses
will be mashed and dispersed Tibetan-style;
then sifters among our leavings may wonder
at marble fragments where Modern Man
chipped a bare claim to personality,
seek to make fit a few cryptic additions
like "Corporal C.A.O.C." or "Master
Mariner" and 'Home is the Hunter."
Meanwhile they are reminders to the living,
our dogs' ecstatic signal-ground
or just touch off mordant reflection–
especially in this section called Pleasant View
on which the stones wittily turn their behinds ...

BARN-WALL BILLS, 1884

When Frank A. Robbins' grand New Circus
Steamed into Bridgetown in 'eighty-four
Everything amazing was there...
Queen Sarbro's Sword-ladder Ascension,
A Tattooed Lady–from Head to Foot
(Was the crowd allowed to see the lot?)
The Only Woolly Elephant in Captivity
(Or could it be the last of the mammoth line?)
Ten Peerless Lady Celebrities and–
Her initial letters since torn away
–Okh, the exotic *Princess of Delhi:*
All transported by rail upon its own
Palatial Trains of *specially constructed*
Cars--but what we most have missed
Was *Burnell's Three-Headed Songstress,*
Otherwise *Warbler,* pictured armless
With three gilt lockets to her dress,
Crepe roses in her/their tripled curls
And one at her standard breast ...
Surely those heads held a single thought,
But did she/they trill as one or three?
How did Burnell fake her, could we have seen
A teetering imposture in the ring?
Or was she precariously posed
In shadowed booth, behind gauzy screen?
Who believed, or were none deceived?
Fancy fails, but who wouldn't sport fifty
Cents to stare, with the buggy-born gawpers
At Bridgetown in that barn-decked century?

(The Nova Scotia Museum)

STORM

The antenna quivers in a nor'-wester–
minus thirty plus a wind-chill factor–
yet draws down Holst's Planets
direct from Roy Thomson Hall,
"Live to Air" in the poetics of stereo,
harmonising the greater, infinite cold.
This hi-tech box transmits all–
but not my fear
as inches from my ear
the gale assaults the wall.
The compelled eye cringes
at an unfrosted pane, spies
snow-glitter
wrenched spruce
anxious fence,
nature's music all percussive:
mind could let go, open a door
into the night, walk unclothed
upon its blanched field of force,
take off to greet planets in flight.

'GULL IN A STORM'

for David Silverberg

Waves
  to make any kind of sea
        gather
and fall.
     A gull can fly over
all
  or downed by storm
will ride
and wait.
     Your eye
    cast him
  in endless flight
  between
seabright   and   blind sky

IN PERSPECTIVE

From a mile in air
snowstorm might appear
puffed sand a foot stirs:

Here below it means
waiting or deadly risk:
huddled house-life peers
till later, in still night
steady ploughs pass whose lights
signal clarity across ceilings;

But in another place
a climber opposed self to storm,
was ripped from the rock-face–
did he, or was he, overcome?

A mile in the air it would all seem
the same, risk or huddle:
what stirred had settled.

VENUS AND THE MOON

Looking up, you could believe
They had arrived
For some purpose in our west:
A crescent moon reclined
With, bright and close
(Not, as knowledge defines,
Two hundred and twenty-five
Times further off in space)
Steady Venus, just outside
Moon's unclasped circlet–
They meant nothing
But chance conjunction,
Yet our eyes clung on
As if to draw down
Those jewels, a possession
Sign and illumination
Past generations had known.

(19 April 1988)

THE SPACE BETWEEN THE STARS

He hovers, trim, on his toes
The raven-suited learned physicist,
To display the gleanings of his years–
And sows an intelligible fact:
Chalks one centimetre apart
In a corner of the board
A dot and a blob, earth and sun,
On which scale, he asserts,
The stretch to our neighbour star
Is 2.7 kilometres–he points
With authority beyond the confines
Of the hall. Our eyes turn
With him and strain at the wall.
A long hour he uttered what few
Could interpret or care for,
Juggled atoms and molecules
Between here and there, then
Carried off his own and his fame.
We scattered across the dark,
Minutely erect, but one who looked up saw
A stupendous cat paw that humourless space.

PRESENCE AND PROCESS

The loved being takes place
in air, whose absence
air ignores...
This evanescent
mystery of presence
suggests how shoots
climb, die, persist:
slight blond grasses
in corners, lee of fence,
drypoint meadowsweet,
hydrangeas'
friable clusters
against snow
though entangled in process
exact minute attention.

STRANDED KEEPSAKE

A sepia pair
Nameless, deframed
On the posthumous shore
of Saturday's Antique Fair;
Signed Alfred Poole, Morecambe,
Who pocketed their sovereign
And invited them to smile:
She, seated, confronts the hooded glare,
But he looks off sidelong as if foreseeing
Where their shared image would land,
Bemused above her braided hair,
Fist clenched in frail male control
On a studio pillar of pasteboard.

BRAVE NEW LOVERS

I saw a stale acquaintance
with a bright new mistress—
glimpsed how fresh was each to the other
and, as he must sometimes do,
sketched around the taut lines
of her face, her trim elastic body,
his wife's ampler form and feature,
the wreck of five times bearing—
and perhaps some rejected image
I cannot see makes incandesce
this new woman's vision of him.
However they survived before,
all lovers inhabit an island,
Miranda sees her Ferdinand;
they would never leave the shore.

MISGIVING

He asked, Would she be kind?
He felt so young, still vital,
But his wife was a cripple–
And was she too not alone?

They need not lie about love,
Pretend to more than need–
Mutual, he felt sure–
But for her it was less simple:

Though he was gentle,
Considerate, pressed no claim,
Her flesh could not collaborate
With her softened heart,
To embrace yet stay compassionate.

WASHROOM SKETCHES

According to that city's *Sun*
fellatio, buggery and masturbation
are charged against thirty males of Orillia–
can this be the little town we once knew
where in public washroom of dim despair
furtive citizens release illicit desire
and policeman in clownish attire
turn voyeur that lawful excretion
pass untainted by the sadly indecent?

(1983)

SUN, MARSH, TRAIN

(1886-1986)

February's glowing sunball
Holds as in a dish
The near snow-sucking marsh
Distant incandescent bay
(Disc of beaten silver)
Rimmed with those dim blue hills:
That "darling illusion" still.

Enter the CN train
Bisecting the scene
Blunt cylinders and oblongs
Floating grids of automobiles–
All we depend upon,
Necessary as the sun
And practically beautiful.

Tantramar

NOTE: This alludes to Sir Charles G. D. Roberts' "Tantramar
    Revisited" (1886).

THE REDNECK

frets in the sticks
of Loyalist N.B.
how the French are taking over a country
the Third World is sucking dry
that English is infected with Aids
that High School students taught
to read filthy books abort–
stamps out to blast a rabbit
or hunches in and punches
with mottled trembling fists
another warning to a rag
nobody reads (the editor
thinks him crazy, gives him space
to make himself ridiculous):
he believes he is an individual,
but there's always another like him,
heir to the congested mind,
a muddled bitter hatred of his kind...

BAGDAD, N.B.

(1989)

Rushing down the TCH
Past Sussex, aiming at Fredericton,
You pass a brown dirt
Sideshoot to Bagdad.
If you brake and follow it
Between ramparts of spruce,
You will come to a place
Of domes and minarets,
Clutching street-markets,
Din of copper-beating alleys,
Shrieking fundamentalists
Summary executions
And a signless plant
Where poison gas is made.

This is of course absurd–
Because if you turn off anywhere
You will inevitably come to Bagdad.

P.S. 1991
This place was formerly Berlin–
They need not change its name again.

PASTORAL ESCAPIST'S VALEDICTION

But it would be very damp, you said:
Yes it would, on an excessively green
Slope of Devon clay, with the thatch
Rain-black, the low-browed sun-denying
Windows and that crooked orchard
Closing in. What did we really fear–
That settled here we would live out
A hollow pastoral, could never go
Erect among its bent labouring ghosts?
Too sentimental: all that mattered was,
It was just our turn, for a brief stay
To walk consciously where they plodded
On the rural roundabout, apt to break back
Or heart if you try to wrest from it
More than it can give: a daffodil slope
Hurts the heart with desiring too much
Merely of things that grow in the soil:
The blue-flashing machine is at the gate–
It was never, you know, a complete retreat.

ESTUARY

Homeward the fisherman across
The grey levels; on this shore
Avocets cluster in swelling mist–
On the other, tree clumps float
Free of earth: a hovering world
Beyond eye's capture borne too fast
In the unnatural train. In these
Turning moments tug the cord,
Dismount and hasten into
The scene. Ignoring their cries
From the false corridor of light,
Enter the grey, become there
The figure you would recall–
One observed, *being*, believing,
Neither in day nor nightfall,
But in permanent presence
Of that momentary scene.
(Near Exmouth)

IN MEMORIAM RESHARD GOOL

(b. London, England, l.10.31, d. P.E.I., 1.5.89)

Not really listening, I overheard
On Stereo Morning's Art Report
A dry summation of your vanished life.
It was just past May Day,
The garden soil warming up–
I hear your rich laugh, what a time
To die, and see again in Rose Valley
That swaying crow drunk on a branch,
Gorged on February's thawed brown apples:
Your laughing self is there still.
When last you 'phoned, I agreed to write
A reference for your living thought,
And yes, we must meet for "chats," life was short;
Soon after, you were massively struck.
Now chances casually foregone hurt
Recall of scattered vital hours...

A cat lay on a green verge that day,
Like Pratt's basking bobcat–
I could not tell whether dead or alive.
It was dead unmarked and I wondered
What point was there in meeting
Two random deaths in a morning?
Your titles were crafty enigmas
The Nemesis Casket, Medusa's Eye
But you believed in meanings
The cracked word might yield;
Poet and scholar "all compact",
The place you chanced to die in
Shrinks back to its insular being.

II

MINOTIS IN 'OEDIPUS COLONEUS'

(At Epidaurus)

Embayed in darkness
fresh-throated bird
soft-governing his chorus,
Minotis
    blinded.
        With what
            the gods sent
Content.

Poetry of the word
        blind words
            seeking
                a word:
Seeing.

                (1961)

OLD MASTER IN A NEW LIGHT

(c. 1610)

In Gentileschi's "David and Goliath"
the lad's toenails are black, every one:
that is realism. He is a street tough,
has lifted Dad's sword from the closet,
has him down and is poised to pay
him out for heavy-fathered adolescence.
It cannot be, you'll surely demur,
what the painter meant, but consider–
it improves on the fanciful notion
that the weak can do in the strong
with a single laser-like hit:
call it a symbolic oedipal act,
a post-scriptural version of fact.

(The Art Gallery, Bath)

'COPPELIA' DECONSTRUCTED

This trifle achieves a lifelike plot:
A handsome young fool
Jilts his girl for a doll;
Had Coppelia been real–
Despair, poison, suicide–
But we know from the start
She is not
While the sparkling jealous dances proceed.

Then in Act Two the blind girl,
Forgiving his fall,
Rushes back to fickle arms
That receive her, not just for her charms,
But because even a fool
                        can distinguish
Between painted wood and flesh...

NOLAN'S 'NED KELLY'

Iconic bushranger
Nolan's iron centaur,
clubbed rifle aslant,
enters the nothing of landscape,
the violated dreamtime:
the oblong aperture
of Kelly's hammered casque
is clouded space...
This arrangement gestures back
to Friedrich's sombrely
contemplative Monk–
the allusion suggests
the Decline of the West:
    sightless will
      confronts
    the firmament.

(The Hayward Gallery, London 1988)

FRANCIS BACON'S POST-CARTESIAN

ANATOMY LESSON

Quivering
    butchered canvases
    tormented enclosures:
    boxed, cubed
    electric-chaired,
    features wrenched;
    baboon grins,
    Isobel Rawsthorne mandril-masked
    dun mattresses
    pustular hanging bulbs
    lavatory bowls;
    Sweeney-Orestes
    carbuncular, goggle-eyed
Scattered
    pilotless vessels,
    visceral
    eviscerated,
    heaped flesh,
    deliquescent
    (Mengele's garbage)
        flesh
Fragmented
    autopsy of exploded being.
                (The Tate Gallery)

THE REACTOR SUITE

Hundreds of images Koop took
distilled to this quartet,
her Reactor Suite:

First two cooling towers rear blind,
black as Browning's in restless water
against a sky flecked sparely
coral upon ashen grey;
next, a sliver of beach
before a sullen shadowed sea,
and a silhouette hunched
in Munch-like despair–
And, standing apart,
a stately great blue heron;
then, alone, like a risen
mutated hammerhead shark,
riding the surface on spread fins,
a sombre nuclear submarine;
and last, two half submerged
humans featureless in the flood.

Only the blue heron is granted
total being–feathered many-
toned grace, with a sentient eye:
nostalgic bird sharing our nemesis,
obsolete its soul-bearing flight
to some fixed firmamental retreat.

NOTE: *The Reactor Suite*, by Wanda Koop (1985) is in the Contemporary Canadian collection at the National Gallery of Canada.

NOT ABOUT KANDINSKY

or, THE ABSTRACTED LOVERS

Have you noticed how
at exhibitions when the young
pause to kiss, the paintings
turn away? Such lovers
subdue the blistering spaces,
skim footsore floors
with a wonderful elan ...

While orthodox art-lovers peer
in brow-creased deconstruction
of Composition IV, Improvisation 29
and *Ohne Titel* Unlimited–
or must with covert glances
skirt canvases the pair
monopolize in abstracted embrace:
so a discreet ballet forms
about their dual Self Portrait.

We are distracted from Kandinsky,
His bursting, fragmented silence.
At last they partly disengage
and slip out of this poem
into the Twenties Room,
drift entwined toward
that Ideal Composition
Painters poets lovers imagine.

Will they ask, Do you remember,
turning a faded Catalogue wonder
what they made of it back in '89?

Or will they, with happy recall,
be painting this poem still?

Schirn Kunsthalle, Frankfurt
June 1989

USELESS?

Acid rain fills Giverny pool,
stipples thought of Monet's lilies
     (thirty paintings
     in sixty days)

Why the hell, he demanded, should I,
Cast up on a bourgeois age,
     Bother to paint?
Yet multiplied his lilies
throughout The Great Carnage:

     Did all that pain
     Somehow affirm
     Water-lily toil?

BEFORE THE DELUGE: THREE VIGNETTES

1. Voltaire's Temperature

On each anniversary of the butchery
of St. Bartholomew's Day, the humane
rational Voltaire felt it all again:
burned with fever for the *fanatisme*
though the blood had long since drained from the Seine;
free thought, he philosophised, would banish
such ills, but could he have lived
two centuries more, he would day after day
have sweated to scale impossible heights
of vicarious anguish...

2. Dvorak on the Bridge

From a bridge in the station at Prague
Dvorak collected the numbers of trains;
his agreeable son-in-law Josef Suk,
as befitted the lesser composer, took
them down. O enviable diversion,
simple and young as discovering
in the country of Manifest Destiny
a resounding New World Carnegie Hall
could believe:
            in Czechoslovakia unborn
(to be still-born in yet a newer world)
steam jetted up under the bridge
shrouded train-spotting Dvorak where he stood,
chanting for Josef his newest numbers,
a notation of innocuous harmonies.

3. Heidegger in '33

Martin Heidegger, whom Being
deathwardly perturbed,

lapsed infamously when Time
was most real. Addressed
Hitler's brown-booted New Men
and authorised all they knew--
Earth and Blood
and *Deutsches Volk*:
withdrawing soon to the Black Forest
of *Dasein*, made philosophical gain,
but involuntarily proved, in '33,
authentic choice between wood and tree.

'NOT ABOUT HEROES'

(On a performance, at Taunton, of Stephen MacDonald's Play)

Between lunch and tea
ices and the anticipated
                    patisserie
two earnest young men
too young to have worn
khaki in earnest–
walk and talk,
talk and recite, enact
Owen and Sassoon
Sassoon and Owen...
We murmur knowing cliches
about what they saw,
made others see
though poems stop no wars.

It all ends in heavy darkness,
blank out on the crouching Owen
whose spilt brave life sucks light
from the bleak, lingering Sassoon.
Outside, a blue-wash January sky;
a tense mother plucks at her son
flinging crumbs to ducks on the River Tone.

WAR GAMES

The boys advance across greying snow,
Menace with shrill unbroken voices,
Fire and fall–it seems no time ago
We kept the real thing from them. Now
They should know and will not listen:
They are killers enough for their need–
Perhaps what they win with solemn
Passionate simulated force
Is the unarmed combat we have lost.

ON READING RATUSHINSKAYA'S 'NO, I'M NOT AFRAII

I would find it difficult to say which is the best environment
for poetic creation—the West, where people have enough to eat, or
the concentration camp, where everyone goes hungry. IGOR GERASCHENKO

A Western poet knuckles his brow
and sweats to imagine a poetic
oppression: solitude of freezing
punishment cell, companioned only
by the mind that spins lines
of hope out of utter deprivation—
how dawnlight conjures rainbows
in the deep-iced high window;
small comradeship of crumb-seeking mouse
who accepts this hole as the universe.
So the huddled chill poet scratches words
upon the threatened mind where they will die
or remarkably in this frost preserved
shoot into print in that other hemisphere
where all can read, many admire
a spirit tempered by enviable conflict,
guiltless brave lyrics all critics praise...
Pity the Western poet as he chokes upon
his free world's tangled lesser evils,
the commonplace anguish of sickness and loss,
or the shame of personal happiness.

(1986)

PRISONER OF CONSCIENCE

for Maina wa Kinyatti

Inconceivably remote from us
who squeeze minutes out to pen
reproving letters to hard statesmen,
light barbed symbolic candles,
the strong defier endures
six solitary years; his cell
should glow with the aura
of every imagined angel:
such martyrs ascend
transcend in their being
all schemes of death or grace.

Their self-shining burns us.

THIS WEEK'S MAJOR POET

"Innovative," "disturbing," they billed him—
Though gentle by nature, one saw,
Itching to declaim some original flaw:

Metred in beard and syllabic denims,
Spills haversacked slim volumes,
Selects at careful random—

At first hardly reads, communes:
Fingers latched in hip pockets,
Poised for the draw—

Then blood, cracked bones, violation
Heaped in steaming images
Across the impervious lectern—

Pauses, tears off sweater,
Rolls checkshirt elbow-tight
Piles on assorted sex and shit—

How they love him now, a man:
Brass-buckled broad leather-belt
(In lace-trailing, climbing boots

A stench of feet down there)—
Climactic fingers with savage grace
Repel plunging black surf of hair—

"Thank you." Delighted to understand,
They give themselves a loud hand.
A disturbance has been created.

PSYCHIC POET

For Jay Ramsay

He speaks, utters
scriptless, bare
throat thrums
fine fingers flex–
slightly embodied
word-medium.
Word beyond words
taps the flow
of waves' motion,
self-absorbed in one,
slow exploding calyx:
and in the arc'd circuit
of reflexive human love
the root of a woman's
sun-reaching stem,
selved with otherness
without and within...

Such poems never end
but pause, concede
to provisional time–
where they turn their glasses,
clap in the vacuum
of unimpassioned attention,
mask the rebuke the faithless feel–
yet, beyond irony, what has poetry ever been
but another awakening someone imagines?

DREAMS OF FAIR WOMEN

The death of that stout incompatible
Cyclist he knew too well
Set Hardy free
To court posthumously
The flashing phantom horsewoman
In flaming elegy
(Iliads of verse
Have sprung from less);
Dickens slew Dora, else
She had ballooned into Kate;
Tied to a frump, Conrad let his quill
Tickle an obsession of oriental girls–

The moral here (for an artist's wife)
Is to notice how art improves life...

ALAS, POOR HIGNETT!

Where, wrote Hignett to Great Hardy,
gnarled with honoured years,
may I place my fiction of sixty
thousand words and these verses?
Only, vouchsafed the Name
"with thanks" by submitting
your MS. to a suitable publisher
and asking his terms: fair
but frosted words. Alas,
Hardy's editors note,
no works of Hignett
ever achieved print–

Poor Hignett, yet that name,
forever enambered in Hardy's reply,
will cling to his gleaned Remains.

SIDNEY SCHOLAR FALLEN AT FIFTY-TWO

He fell beside his books,
a general upon the field;
no intimation of mortality
had been remarked: he had
breakfasted well, driven
to the Institute, urbanely
informed a respectful seminar,
the routine of twenty-five years.
His text was always the Renaissance,
all since mere afterbirth. Our age
offered him no such ultimate moment
as that humane aristocratic gesture
of his poet fallen on the field of Zutphen,
resigning the cup to a pikeman...
So dying, he missed his life's
perfect conjunction, speaking upon
his man's four-hundreth
in suedes, subtle checks and polo-neck.

HINDU TRACES

I. CEMETERY, SINGAPORE

The paupers' graves preserve mute art
To move: rash mound and numbered concrete
Block–businesslike and neat.
More prosperous corpses bear dead weight
Of stuccoed brick or marbled debt–
Peel crack fade, prodigiously depreciate:

All impartially commemorate
With joss-sticks, acrid, purple
In a coca-cola bottle.

II. ROADSIDE SHRINE, MALAYA

This is a holy spot–a lean-to
tumbled in the lee of a convex corner
where fumes of hectic scooters gather:
The Image a concrete lump on a ledge--
no form–a foolish pug-dog's face,
a flake of paint clings to the lip;
rods well-rusted remind of arms–
confetti of candle-droppings surround
the vanished feet. From the rafters
swings a tarnished copper burner
bestowing snatches of sacred aroma:
a thing Indians here kneel before,
    Here is India.

TO AN INDIVIDUALIST

Belonging to no place or nation,
you have lived out of time
and called it freedom.
Yet time is not what others do:
it carries you
on, not through–
and monstrously impersonal age
imprints the separate face
in any crowd,
staring out, incredulous.

'SWANS STILL AT COOLE'

(Newspaper Report)

Yes, there are swans still at Coole
But the great house has gone:
Now, unleashed, the "base-born"
Tread those precious spirits' gravel,
Bawl at their kids
Thrusting bread at birds
Whose sudden bite
Recalls that wing-haired poet.

PIGEON POLITY BEFORE EXETER CATHEDRAL

As if keeping time to an inner tune
The pigeons lift off the Cathedral Green
And whirl the arc of the timbered fronts
And dip below the west cliff of netted
Monarchs, and then, as of one wavering
Mind, go high again toward the quick sky,
Blobs dashed against the clouds' canvas,
And having wheeled a final round,
Drop to march about the green ground,
Jerkily assertive, plump and graceless;
One, as always, claims and limes the bonnet
Of Richard Hooker, the judicious divine,
Who appears resigned to the old canard
That his reason bowed to a henpecking wife,
Sat upon by birds in death as in life.

BIRDS OF HONG KONG

No wonder the Chinese love caged birds:
Needing neither sun nor breeze
They seem to rejoice in tiny domed worlds;
Mechanic din and many-mouthed Cantonese
Cannot still their voice–
The budgerigar goes sweetly on
Even in a clanking tram.
Your taxi, for two dollars,
Carries "any animal or bird."
Their owners, seething in concrete nests
Whose neighbours thieve all light
Buy creatures to do their singing for them.

And I could mark, looking down
At dawn from the Emerald Hotel's
Nineteenth floor how the stained square
That tops a mere fourteen floors below
Would suddenly blossom with seed:
Some quick vertiginous hand
I never caught supplies the wheeling
Fan-tailed pigeons, in boxes and baskets
Set out beneath clustered antennae;
The hand knows these creatures,
Though free of air and ledges,
Are compelled to a space of order
And peace by its regular
Constraining service: so perfection
Coos and sings unaware of limitation.

THE DISARMING 'LANGUAGE OF THE BIRDS'

(from The Mantiq al Tayr, School of Bihzad, Iran 1483)

Eight assorted birds stand in a cleft
among billowing hills, over which
a hunter peers, finger to his lips,
long gun shouldered, slanting
far beyond the painting's border:
it is called "The Language of the Birds."

But what is it they are saying–
This being with the firestick means
us harm? (Firestick, I say, as if
their marvellous utterance were
human mimicry: their language,
naturally, would be avian...)

Still, whatever they are saying,
their enemy stands disarmed,
finger at mouth and will not,
surely, shatter such converse:
who would wish to silence
        creatures so gifted–
unless, of course, they be men?

EN ROUTE TO MALTA

13 May 1804

The poet watched from the deck
sailors shoot at a drooping hawk
which could find no rest on wave
or bowsprit of any other vessel,
for it was everywhere a mark.

The poet's note does not reveal
he protested at what he deemed, not cruel,
but a thoughtless failure to feel;
yet we know in his remarkable Rime
of 'ninety-eight he made such acts a crime:

The poet perhaps reflected that real men
with smoking guns would not just then
      stay to hear some absurd
      yarn wedding man and bird.

HORSE / MAN

For centuries man urged the horse
into his wars, made in armour
with him a deadly double beast:
upon coin and temple
the horse engraved tramples
the lion (no friend to man),
suffers with liquid glance
the final envious lance
or claw:
      no use wondering
what horses made of this–
they will, it seems, bend
to every use man exacts:
will bear race course and prance
in fear, contest or blinkered faith,
man's slave servant friend god
or flesh for rites of slaughter.

Man's need of them is egoism
but what is theirs of him?

LAB. LANGUAGE

(A Euphemistic Exercise)

In the scholarly paper, how abstract
Is the suffering of the rat–
Which henceforth we shall call "the participant":
Shut in a lightless cabinet,
But fed and punctually cleansed,
Drawn open regularly to receive
Subcutaneous measures of morphine--
This we describe as "conditioning".
Then there is the hot-plate technique:
Sixty seconds at fifty centigrade
Yields "paw-licking" notations–
So furnishing data on "tolerance."
Such is the language deployed to record
This creatures's choiceless participation.

ACID ODE FOR THE OLD WORLD

Still glides the stream, and shall for ever glide;
The Form remains, the Function never dies.
　　　　　　"Valediction for the River Duddon"

Daily down the autobahn
from Black Forest retreats
commute the miraculous knights
whose Mercedean exhalations
choke firs their windshields admire;
the "blue miracle" of Chartres
has curdled; only Lord Elgin's
fortunate theft saved
those Marbles of the Parthenon
from turning Grecian gypsum.
Flesh of stone dissolves,
gouged by anti-rains
that neither renew nor cleanse.

What must this mean for poetry
which ploughed and built, believed
what was well made endures,
not only in Old World structures
but deeper in the wilderness
we dream of: our murderous
cosmic fall-out corrodes
the peaks of vision—
climb to the high blue tarn
and count the poisoned trout—
that mirroring lake is a lethal solution:
the sky-line pine
you see float there
gasps at its root.
Mist and wind turn killing chemists,
renew retribution for the albatross.
Now, no more wishful verses

wedding man and nature
in "holy passion" et cetera:
Wordsworth surely knew,
doddering by the Duddon,
that already black stew
of Irwell and Don crawled
through Manchester and Sheffield
a day south of his Lakes;
Poetry must now know it loves
a body turned cancerous,
blow hard the late alert
to cleanse the real earth
whose imagined presences
her ruthless rain dissolves.